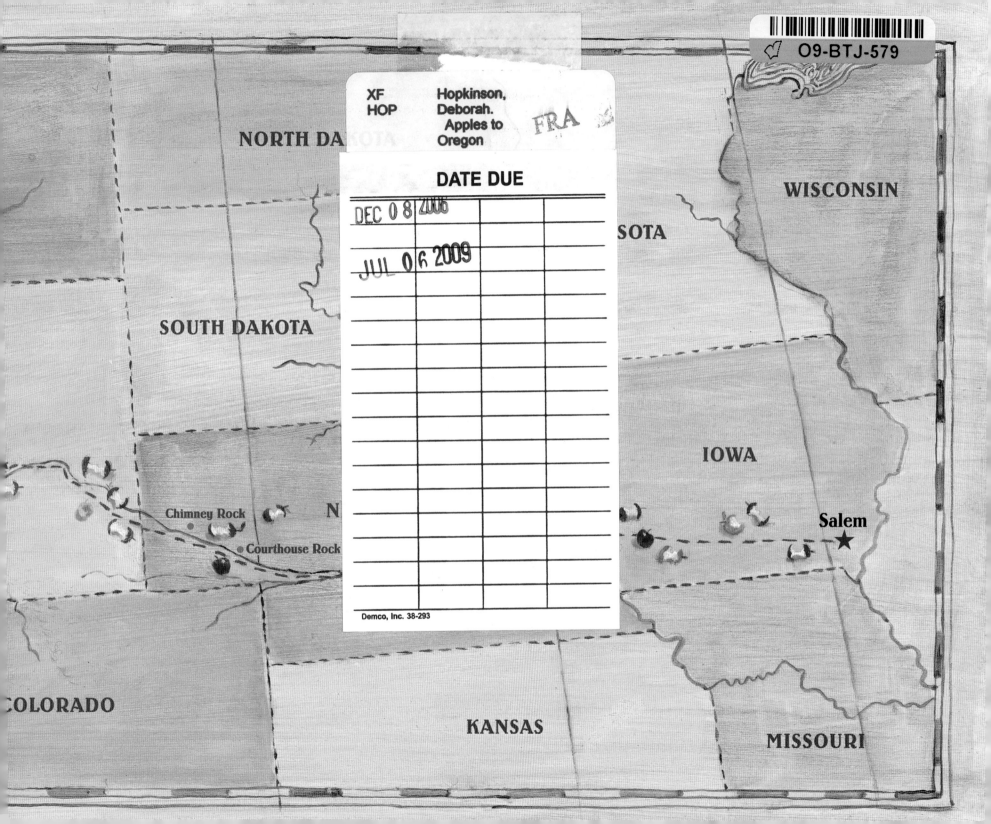

BY DEBORAH HOPKINSON

# APPLES TO

Being the (Slightly) True

Narrative of How a Brave

Pioneer Father Brought

Apples, Peaches, Pears, Plums,

Grapes, and Cherries

(and Children)

Across the Plains

ILLUSTRATED BY NANCY CARPENTER

# OREGON

ATHENEUM BOOKS FOR YOUNG READERS

New York    London    Toronto    Sydney

For my favorite Oregon girls:
Keelia, Meghan, and Aili Johnston, who'll go far, even wearing one boot
—D. H.


For my aunt Caryl, who sends apples, pears, and peaches from
Oregon year-round, and for my husband, Kevin, who leaves a trail
of apple cores wherever he goes
—N. C.

Background information for this story was gathered from various sources, including a pamphlet called "The Beginnings of the Apple Industry in Oregon," written by Joseph W. Ellison and reprinted from *Agricultural History*, Volume 11, October 1937; and the "Luelling-Campbell Family History and Genealogy," a typescript manuscript compiled by Jane Harriet Luelling and housed at Oregon State University.

Atheneum Books for Young Readers
An imprint of Simon & Schuster
Children's Publishing Division
1230 Avenue of the Americas, New York, New York 10020
Text copyright © 2004 by Deborah Hopkinson
Illustrations copyright © 2004 by Nancy Carpenter
All rights reserved, including the right of reproduction
in whole or in part in any form.
Book design by Lee Wade
The text of this book is set in Regula.
The illustrations are rendered in oil paint.
Manufactured in China

4 5 6 7 8 9 10
Library of Congress Cataloging-in-Publication Data
Hopkinson, Deborah.

Apples to Oregon: being the (slightly) true narrative of how a brave pioneer father brought apples, peaches, pears, plums, grapes, and cherries (and children) across the plains/ by Deborah Hopkinson ; illustrated by Nancy Carpenter.    p. cm.
Summary: A pioneer father transports his beloved fruit trees and his family to Oregon in the mid-nineteenth century. Based loosely on the life of Henderson Luelling.
ISBN 0-689-84769-6
[1. Fruit trees—Fiction. 2. Apples—Fiction. 3. Frontier and pioneer life—Fiction. 4. Overland journeys to the Pacific—Fiction. 5. Tall tales.] I. Carpenter, Nancy, ill. II. Title.
PZ7.H778125 Ap 2003
[E]—dc21
2001022949

My daddy loved growin' apples. And when he got ready to pull up roots and leave Iowa for Oregon, he couldn't bear to leave his apple trees behind.

So Daddy built two of the biggest boxes you could ever hope to see. He set them into a sturdy wagon and shoveled in good, wormy dirt. Then he filled every inch with little plants and trees. Hundreds of them!

Daddy was ready for the most daring adventure in the history of fruit.

"Apples, ho!" he cried.

Along with apples, my daddy took peaches, pears, plums, grapes, and cherries.

Oh, and by the way, he took us along too.

We all had lots to do on the journey. Each morning I helped Momma bake biscuits, while Daddy prepared for another long day on the trail. At night Momma and I tucked in the little ones, then Daddy fiddled lullabies under the stars. Why, I can still hear him crooning to the Gravensteins,

"Hush, little babies, don't you cry
Momma's gonna bake you in an apple pie.
If that apple pie ain't sweet,
Daddy's gonna munch you for his own special treat."

We rolled along just fine till we came to the Platte River. It was wider than Texas, thicker than Momma's muskrat stew, and muddier than a cowboy's toenails. Just looking at it made my insides shrivel.

The riverbank was crowded with folks in prairie schooners trying to get up the nerve to cross.

When they saw us and all our little fruit trees fluttering in the breeze, they burst out laughing.

"Those leaves will be brown as dirt before you hit the plains," declared one old geezer.

"Plains?" scoffed someone else. "That nursery wagon won't make it halfway across the river."

But Daddy didn't let their talk worry him. He just looked me square in the eye and said, "Delicious, I'm gonna need your help."

Right then and there we built a raft for his tiny trees, then Daddy loaded me and my little sisters and brothers onto the edges.

"Now, make sure my precious plants don't topple into the water," Daddy warned.

Well, we hadn't gone far when that muddy drink
started to pull us down.

"The peaches are plummeting!" my sisters shouted.

"The plums are plunging!" boomed my brothers.

## "Don't let my babies go belly-up!" howled Daddy.

I had to think quick. "We're too heavy. If we don't go faster, we'll sink. We gotta take our shoes off and kick!"

And so we kicked.

'Course we'd all been raised on apples, and everyone knows young 'uns raised on apples are strong, mighty strong. Before you could say "Johnny Appleseed," we'd kicked ourselves clear to the other shore.

But no sooner had we got every last tree loaded back in the wagon than I spied a foul-looking bunch of clouds stomping round the sun just fit to be tied.

The wind began to throw around everything that wasn't lashed down—our boots, baby Albert's diapers, every pot and pan Momma had, even our own little wagon.

Next, hailstones big as plums came hurtling out of the sky.

"Guard the grapes! Protect the peaches!" Daddy howled.

So we all started tearing off our clothes and holding them over Daddy's darlings. Bonnets, petticoats, trousers, hats—even Daddy's drawers!

**Whew!** At last the storm passed and Daddy's dainties were safe.

After all that excitement it felt good to hit the trail again. But before long we came to an endless sandy desert. Now remember, us young 'uns didn't have our wagon or our boots. In no time our feet were redder than the poison apple the old witch gave to Snow White.

"Delicious, this is our toughest challenge," said Daddy, wiping his brow as I followed him on tippy toes. "We got to find a water hole or my babies are done for."

Sure enough, by noon the fruit trees began to droop. By three their itty-bitty tender leaves were getting crispy. By nightfall Daddy was crying, a handful of dead branches pressed against his heart.

I couldn't bear to see my daddy suffer. So early next morning I took off to look for water. But although I searched and searched, I couldn't even find a splash or a puddle.

After a while I got so tuckered out, I plopped down under an old sagebrush.

"Ouch!" I yelled, landing on something hard. But when I saw what it was, I whooped for joy. My very own boot! What's more, it still had some water in it from all those melted hailstones.

That was our lucky day, let me tell you. We found every one of Momma's pots and pans spread out across the sand. They all had a few drops of water in them too. Just enough to get Daddy's trees to the next water hole before they all keeled over.

My, that first sip of water sure tasted good, even if I did have to wait my turn behind some Baldwin apples.

Oh, and I'm pleased to say our wagon and all the boots turned up too.

All except one.

I reckon that nasty wind blew my left boot clear to the other side of the moon. And if it should happen to drop out of the sky on your head one of these days, I'd sure appreciate your sending it along to me.

Well, we kept on going, past Courthouse Rock and Chimney Rock and Independence Rock and lots of other rocks that didn't have names. We climbed up rocks and down rocks. And at last we reached the Columbia River.

"Just a hundred miles to go," declared Daddy.

But time was running out. Our little trees had almost drowned in the river, got pounded by hailstones, and got withered by drought. How much more could they take?

And now we were set for a showdown with the most ornery varmint of all: Jack Frost.

Oh, I'd already spied him sneaking around our campsite, brushing the cottonwoods with his cold white tongue. But I wasn't about to let him get close to my daddy's apples.

So that night I made a big fire and sat by it, waiting for Jack Frost to show himself. Sure enough, as soon as the moon came up I spotted that ole good-for-nothing slinking across the meadow, heading straight for the Sweet Junes.

I got ready to fight. Jack Frost came at me, turning the ground so cold my toes went numb. But I didn't give up.

I grabbed a flaming stick and threw it right at him. Before you could say "Peter Piper picked a peck of pretty pippins," that low-down scoundrel was hightailing it out of there, heading straight for Walla Walla, Washington.

"I'm mighty grateful, Delicious," said Daddy as he scrutinized his
sweeties the next morning. "Thanks to you, even the Sweets stayed snug."
"We were nice and cozy too," added Momma, checking the children.

Sure enough, all Daddy's trees survived, just as if they'd come across the plains in a swanky carriage. We floated them on boats down the mighty Columbia to a pretty place near Portland.

Then we planted them in that sweet Oregon dirt at last.

Gold was discovered in California not long after, and thousands of people rushed there to seek their fortunes.

But not us. We already had our fortune. Those apples, peaches, pears, plums, grapes, and cherries made us richer than any prospector.

We were happier, too. After all, apples taste a whole lot better than gold.

As for my daddy, he was always sweet as a peach. He and Momma lived happily to a ripe old age.

Daddy never forgot my brave deeds on the trail. Why, as soon as he sold his first bushel of apples, he bought me the prettiest pair of boots you ever saw.

"Delicious," said Daddy, "you'll always be the apple of my eye."

# AUTHOR'S NOTE

Although *Apples to Oregon* is mostly a tall tale, the first apple trees really did come to Oregon in a wagon. In 1847 a pioneer named Henderson Luelling (also spelled Lewelling) left Salem, Iowa, with his wife, Elizabeth, and eight children (Alfred, Mary, Asenath, Rachel, Jane, Hannah, Levi, and Albert), and a wagon carrying seven hundred plants and young fruit trees.

Finding water for the "traveling nursery" on the journey must have posed a challenge. When the family reached the town of The Dalles on the Columbia River, the trees were put on boats to be taken downriver. The family settled in Milwaukie, about six miles south of Portland, Oregon, where they planted Oregon's first orchard. Their ninth child, a boy named Oregon Columbia, was born soon after they arrived. The Luelling-Meek Nursery, established together with Henderson's brother, Seth, and William Meek, has been called the "mother of Oregon nurseries." Seth is also credited with introducing the Bing cherry, in honor of a Chinese foreman who worked in his orchard. The Seth Lewelling School in Milwaukie, Oregon, is named for him.

Although some people thought that Mr. Luelling had a crazy idea, it turned out to be not so crazy after all. He made a profit of seventy-five dollars from the first box of apples sold in Portland, and it's said that a bushel shipped to California gold miners fetched five hundred dollars! Today fruit orchards remain an important part of Oregon's economy.

There are hundreds of varieties of apples, and new ones are being developed all the time. (My favorite new apple is called Honeycrisp.) Some of the varieties mentioned in this story are ones Mr. Luelling brought with him. But though the narrator is named Delicious (I just couldn't resist that name!), Golden Delicious apples weren't introduced until after the turn of the century.

# ILLUSTRATOR'S NOTE

My favorite apple is the Winesap.

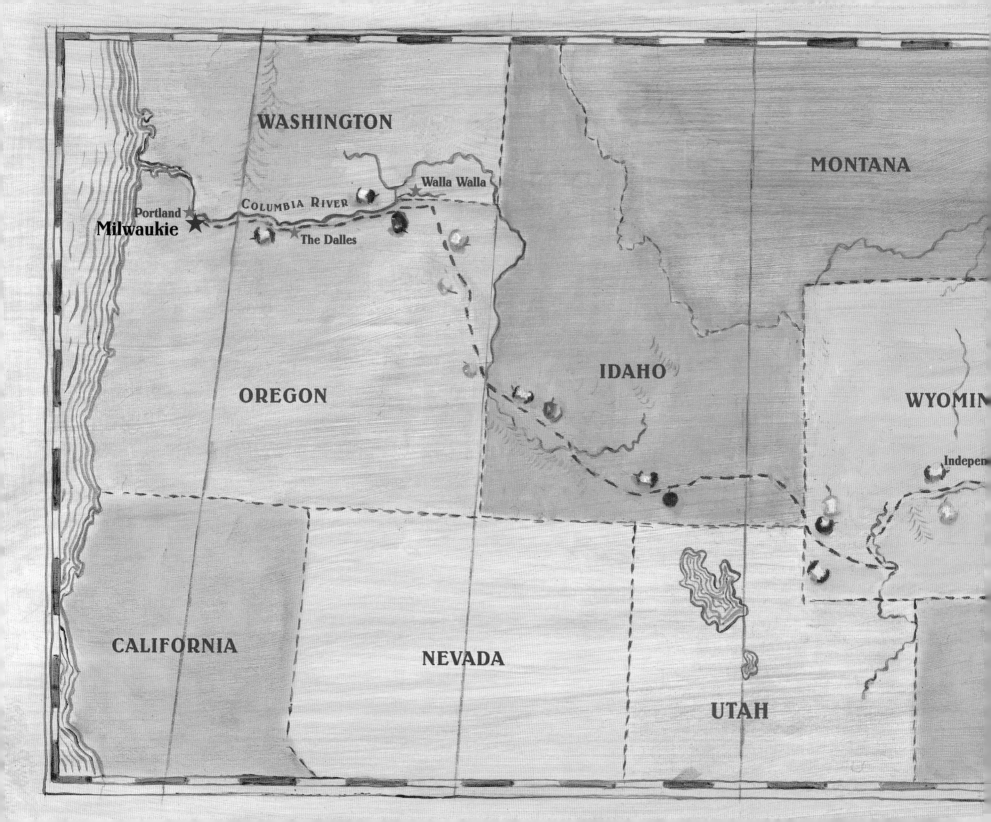